# Real True Friends

## by

## Jean Ure

## Illustrated by Charlie Alder

First published in 2012 in Great Britain by
Barrington Stoke Ltd
18 Walker St, Edinburgh, EH3 7LP

www.barringtonstoke.co.uk

ISBN: 978-1-78112-078-1

Printed in China by Leo

# Contents

# Chapter 1
# The Queen of Cool

Last year, Mum and Dad got divorced. Me and Mum had to move house. We ended up in a tiny little flat on the far side of the country. It was miles away from everything I was used to.

"I'm so sorry, Hannah!" Mum said. "I know this must be hard for you, but it's all we can afford."

I tried not to grumble cos I knew that it was hard for Mum too. But I hated the fact I had to start at a new school, and in the middle of term as well.

Mum tried her best to comfort me. "You're still only in Year 7," she said. "People won't have had time to get to know each other yet."

She might have been right if it had been the winter term. But it wasn't – it was spring. By the time you get to spring term everyone is settled into their own cosy little group, with their own special friends. If anyone comes from outside, they're like, "Who's this? What's she doing here?"

Poor Mum! She was almost as nervous as I was. She kept saying, "Edenbridge is a really good school! I promise, Han, it won't take you long to make friends."

I knew she felt bad that she and Dad had split up. But there wasn't any need! It wasn't like I blamed her. If I blamed anyone, I blamed Dad. In any case, splitting up is just one of those things – a fact of life. I could have been grown up about it, if only we hadn't had to move!

"You made friends at St Mary's fast enough," Mum said.

But St Mary's had been different. At St Mary's, we'd all been new together. At Edenbridge I felt like I was some kind of alien. Like I just didn't belong.

At the end of the first week, Mum asked me how I was getting on. I wanted to burst into tears and wail, "I hate it, I hate it!" But that would have upset Mum, so I just mumbled, "OK, I suppose." I hoped she would leave it at that, but Mum knows me too well.

She gave me a hug and said, "Be brave, Han! Things will get better, I promise."

I muttered that I didn't think so.

"It'll be fine," Mum said. "I give you my word."

"But nobody talks to me!" The words burst out before I could stop them. "It's like I'm not even there!"

"Well, now, that's easy to solve," Mum said. "If they won't talk to *you*, you could just go and talk to them. Don't be shy – they won't bite! They're only people, the same as you. Just go up and say something!"

But how could I? I was the new girl! It wasn't up to me to speak to them, it was up to them to speak to me. And they didn't want to know. They thought I was odd, cos I came from another part of the country and I talked weird. Like it was my fault how I talked!

There was only one girl who took any notice of me. She was called Zoe Frost. I was behind her one day in the lunch line. I watched as she picked up a packet of biscuits and began to read the writing on it. She turned to me and shook her head.

"Nuts," she said.

"N-nuts?" I said.

"I can't eat them," she said. "I have this allergy. Even just a crumb would make me swell up like a balloon."

I said, "Oh!" It was all I could think of to say.

Zoe peered at the packet of biscuits again. "I always have to read the labels. You'd be surprised at the number of things that have nuts in them. See? Look!" She waved the biscuits at me. "Nut traces! I knew it!"

I asked her what would happen if she ate the biscuits by mistake. She looked at me with big eyes and said, "I'd probably die."

I thought this must be kind of scary for her. I also thought that maybe I would be brave and go and sit at her table so that we could chat some more. I was so happy that someone had taken notice of me!

Then a voice hissed in my ear. "Her and her stupid nut allergy!"

I turned to see who it was. *Michelle Morrison!* I was so surprised I almost dropped my tray.

Michelle was, like, the Queen of Cool. She was the girl everyone wanted to be friends with. And now she was talking to me! To *me!*

"She's totally mad," said Michelle. She reached across for a packet of biscuits and took the same one Zoe had put back.

"These are my favourites," she said.

The biscuits were pink wafers with cream inside. Yum! They were my favourites, too. I looked to see if there were any more, but all that was left were boring flapjack things.

"Sorry!" Michelle put the biscuits down on her tray. "Last one! I suppose I have to thank old Freaky for that."

Freaky was what she called Zoe. I'd heard her do it before. I tried hard to think of something to say in reply.

"She can't eat them," I said. "They've got nut traces in."

"Ow, wow!" Michelle went into a pretend swoon. "Nut traces!"

"She said they could kill her."

"Yeah, right!" Michelle rolled her eyes. "Some people will say anything. You don't want to take any notice of Zoe Frost."

# Chapter 2
# Boffin Brain

I made up my mind that Michelle was right – I didn't want to take any notice of Zoe Frost. Zoe was, like, the class freak. She looked odd, for a start. Her hair was all mad and messy, and her teeth stuck out. Plus she had this huge big brain.

"She always thinks she knows everything," Michelle grumbled.

People don't like it when someone knows everything. If I knew all the answers in every class I would try to hide it a bit. I wouldn't put my hand up every single time. I would pretend, just now and again, that I was the same as everyone else.

Zoe didn't seem to think like that. Maybe she didn't understand that if you want to be popular, you have to work at it. Or maybe she just didn't care.

But I did! I wanted to be popular. It was Michelle's gang that I had to get into – Michelle, Candy Lim and Ivana Smith. They were the cool ones! I could have nothing more to do with Zoe.

It was kind of sad, cos I did quite like her. It's hard *not* to like the first person who has made an effort to speak to you in a new school. I made up my mind that I wouldn't ignore Zoe. If she said something to me, I would say something back. And if she came and sat next to me in class, I wouldn't move away or anything. That would be rude. It would also be unkind. I didn't want to be unkind. I just didn't want to be labelled as a friend of the freak!

Michelle always called Zoe 'Freaky Frost', so that was what I started calling her, too. I said to Mum one day, "There's this girl in my class, Zoe Frost. We call her 'Freaky'."

"That's not very nice," said Mum.

I told Mum that we didn't do it to her face. "But she's really odd! Like, she has this thing where she can't eat nuts. She says they make her swell up."

"Poor girl," said Mum. "Nut allergies can be very dangerous."

I said, "Yeah, right, she could drop dead."

Mum looked at me. "Do you think that's funny?"

I turned a bit pink, then, because of course it wasn't funny. I'd just been showing off in front of Mum. To let her know there was someone who was even less cool than I was.

A few days later, Mum asked me if I'd managed to make any friends yet. My heart pounded a bit as I said that I had. "Michelle Morrison. She's, like, the leader of this group. Her and two others, they all hang around together."

Mum said, "And you're one of them?"

"Well, sort of," I said.

Mum was so pleased! She said, "Well done. I knew you'd get there!"

In fact it was the most terrible lie. Michelle hadn't even looked at me since that day in the lunch line. Zoe was the only person who ever talked to me. I was just as much on my own as I had ever been.

One day after school I was waiting at the bus stop and Michelle was there, just in front of me. She was talking to a girl called Ellie Daniels. Ellie was in our class. She was a nobody. She went round with other nobodies. She wasn't *anyone*.

I thought that if Michelle was talking to Ellie, it couldn't be anything important. If she had been talking to Candy or Ivana, I wouldn't dream of butting in. But it was only Ellie! So I beamed and said, "Hi!"

They both turned and looked at me. Michelle said, "Hi." Ellie didn't say anything at all. Then they both turned back and went right on talking like I wasn't even there.

The bus came and we all went up to the top deck. Michelle and Ellie sat on the front seat and I sat behind them. I leaned forward so I could hear what they were saying. I wasn't being nosy! I just wanted to join in.

Ellie was going on about one of the teachers, Mr Dearborn. He'd given her a D minus for her English homework.

"D minus!" she wailed. "It's so unfair!"

Michelle said, "Yeah, it was probably worth at least a whole D."

I giggled at that. I mean, I thought it was meant to be funny. Ellie screwed her head round and peered at me like I was a lump of dirt that had fallen off the bottom of someone's shoe. Michelle turned round too. She said, "You want to say something, geek?"

That made me go all red, and hot, and embarrassed. For our English homework we'd had to write essays with the title *Starting Over*. I'd written about starting at a new school. For the first time in my life I got an A plus! Mr Dearborn said, "An excellent piece of work, Hannah." I just wish he hadn't said it in front of the whole class, cos now it looked like I was boasting. Which I wasn't! But I could see that it might seem like I was.

"You and old Freaky," said Michelle. "Pair of show-offs!"

"*Boffin* brain!" hissed Ellie.

For the rest of the way, they both ignored me. I sat there with my cheeks burning. I had to keep swallowing to stop the tears welling into my eyes. I'd done what Mum had said, I'd tried to join in, and now they hated me. They thought I was a show off!  And now Michelle would tell Candy and Ivana, and Ellie would tell everyone else, and nobody would want to come anywhere near me. I was never going

to fit in! I was doomed for all time to be a loser. A freak, like Zoe. A show off!

I didn't know it then, but my life was about to change.

# Chapter 3
# Four-leaf Clover

After tea that night, I went into our tiny little bit of garden and threw myself down on the grass. I was supposed to be doing my homework. That's what I told Mum I was going to do. But instead I found that I was still sniffling and snuffling and trying not to cry. I felt *so* sorry for myself. I hated my new school! Why, why, *why* had Mum and Dad split up?

I dug my fingers deep into the soil of our scrubby little patch of grass. Mum said that you couldn't call it a lawn. "Not with all that clover."

I don't know what's wrong with clover. I like it, I think it's pretty. But then I'm not a gardener.

I looked at a clump of it, growing just nearby. And that was when I saw it – a clover with four leaves. A four-leaf clover! I pulled it up and raced indoors.

"Mum!" I yelled. "Look!"

I held it out in my cupped hands.

"Oh, lucky you," said Mum. "You'll have to make a wish on that!"

I closed my eyes and I made my wish. I wished for a friend ... a real, true friend.

"Done?" said Mum.

I nodded. "I don't suppose it'll come true, though. I mean ... it's just a story, like Santa or the tooth fairy, isn't it?"

"Well ... yes and no," said Mum. "Things do sometimes come true, if you want them enough. Just not always in the way you expect."

I didn't really expect anything. I didn't expect to arrive at school next morning and find a real, true friend all ready and waiting. So at least it wasn't a let-down when it didn't happen. Well, not too much of one. Perhaps just a little bit. I'd been kind of having these daydreams where a stunning new girl walked into class and came right over and sat next to me. She would see at a glance that I was the one person above all others she wanted for a friend.

Michelle and her lot would be like, *"Excuse me?"* They would hardly be able to believe it – the amazing new girl choosing boring old Boffin Brain above them!

By first break, when my stunning new friend hadn't turned up, I knew she wasn't ever going to. But it didn't stop my daydreams! As I packed up my books I pretended that she was there, at the empty desk next to me.

Michelle swished past and I smiled at her. Up-beat and confident. She was well surprised! She even smiled back. Well, her lips twitched. It was a sort of smile.

I finished putting my books away and went out into the yard. I dreamed that my new best friend was with me. All of a sudden I felt like a different person. I could go anywhere, I could do anything. I could talk to anyone I liked!

I almost felt brave enough to go and talk to Michelle. She was in a huddle with Candy and Ivana. I could go up to them if I wanted!

Michelle saw me and said something to the others. They all turned to look at me. And then Michelle smiled. Not just a twitch of her lips. A proper smile!

I was about to go over there when Zoe popped up. She said, "Hey, you know that essay you wrote? It was really good!"

I said, "Oh. Thank you." I didn't want to be rude.

"Was it based on fact?" asked Zoe.

I frowned. "It was just an essay."

"It felt like it was based on fact," said Zoe. "That bit about feeling like an alien? That was just how I felt when I first came here."

That surprised me. *"Really?"* I said.

"Really," said Zoe.

"But ... didn't you start at the same time as everyone else?" I said.

Zoe shook her head. "I had to go into hospital." She screwed up her face. "I ate *peanuts*. Not on purpose! They were in this biscuit someone gave me. It was my own fault. I should have been more careful."

I didn't know what to say. I remembered asking Zoe what would happen if she ate a nut by mistake. Zoe had said, "I'd probably die."

I suppose I hadn't really believed her at the time.

"It's scary, isn't it," said Zoe, "when you have to start somewhere new in the middle of a term?"

I agreed that it was. We walked round the yard together, in the sunshine, talking about it. As we walked, I could feel Michelle watching me.

We had Maths first thing after break, and Zoe came and sat by me. At lunch time, she was next to me in the line.

"Don't forget to check for nuts," I said.

Zoe giggled and said, "If I start swelling up, just dial 999!"

I was amazed she could make jokes about it. I thought that was so brave of her.

As soon as lunch was over, Zoe had to rush off to have a piano lesson. Michelle and the others came up to me in the yard.

"You *so* don't want to hang out with old Freaky," said Michelle.

I sighed. "I know, I just felt sorry for her."

The minute I said it, I wished I hadn't. It was mean!

"If you're not careful," said Candy, "you'll get stuck with her."

"Yes, and you don't want *that*," said Michelle.

She slipped her arm through mine and swung off across the yard, pulling me with her. I was one of the gang!

# Chapter 4
## Mystery Celeb

Very soon, it was going to be my birthday. Mum asked me if I'd like to invite a few of my friends for a pizza. "How about this Michelle you were talking about?"

Michelle? I wasn't sure that I would be brave enough. Me, ask the great Michelle Morrison to share my birthday pizza?

Mum saw me hesitate. "Have I put my foot in it?" she said. "Aren't you friends any more?"

I said, "Yes! It's just ... Michelle is, like, really popular, you know?"

"Oh." Mum pulled a face. "I get it! You think she's too grand to come and eat pizza with us."

I said, "Only cos she's so popular. She can't say yes to everything!"

"Do you really want her to come?" said Mum.

I said, "Everybody wants Michelle to come!"

"In that case," said Mum, "why not just try asking her? You never know ... you might get a nice surprise."

And oh, I did! I did! I waited until Zoe wasn't around, then I steeled my nerves and came out with it in a sort of mad rush: "It's my birthday on Saturday, we're going up the road for a pizza, would you like to come?"

"On Saturday?" said Michelle.

"And the others, of course! Candy and Ivana. All of you!"

I could feel my cheeks burn bright pillar box red. But guess what? Michelle said yes! I could hardly believe it. The great Michelle Morrison!

Now I really *was* one of the gang. We hung around together all the time. Zoe still sat next to me in class, but that was just cos we were in the same set for lots of subjects. Michelle jeered and said, "Brains United!"

"I'm not a brain!" I said. "Not like Zoe."

"Yeah, well, whatever you do, don't let her get the idea she can hang out with you," said Candy.

"I won't," I said. "I wouldn't!"

"You don't want people to start thinking you're a freak like her," said Candy. "You know what she told me the other day? She told me she's never seen the Big Game Show!"

The others rolled their eyes, so I rolled mine as well.

Michelle said, "Everyone make sure they watch tonight. You-Know-Who is going to be on!"

Candy and Ivana both squeaked.

Michelle gave me a little shove. "Hannah? Make sure you watch!"

"I will, I will!" I said, and I gave a little squeak of my own.

I wasn't brave enough to ask who You-Know-Who was. I was terrified in case they discovered my dark secret. Zoe wasn't the only one that had never seen the Big Game Show!

"Look out for the Mystery Celeb," said Ivana. "I heard it's a friend of You-Know-Who!"

Candy said, "*No!*"

"That's what I heard," said Ivana.

I said, "Wow!"

The last class of the day was French. I wasn't that good at French, I really wasn't, but I had been put in the top set with Zoe. So, of course, she had to come and plonk herself down beside me. It wasn't my fault! You can't stop people sitting next to you, if that is what they want to do.

Zoe nudged me. She said, "Hey! I've got a book for you." She pulled it out of her bag and slid it across the desk. It had a bright pink cover and was called *Diary of a Teenage Vampire*. Zoe giggled. "She's not really a vampire! She just pretends that she is. It's hilarious!"

HIL-ARI-OUS. That was *such* a Zoe sort of word.

"Trust me," she said, "it's really, really funny. The things that happen to her! Read it and tell me what you think."

I put the book in my bag with my homework. On the bus I took it out and read the bit on the back. It made me giggle. Zoe was right – this book was funny.

After tea I told Mum that I was going to my room to do my homework. "But at eight o'clock," I said, "there's this show I want to watch. The Big Game Show?"

Mum pulled a face. "What on earth do you want to watch that rubbish for?"

I said, "*Mum*! It's not rubbish. There's a mystery celeb and I want to find out who it is."

"I bet it won't be anyone I've ever heard of," said Mum.

"That's because you're not cool."

"No," agreed Mum. "I'm not at all cool."

"You really should make an effort to keep up," I said. "You're not that old."

For some reason, Mum seemed to find this funny.

I finished my homework in half the normal time. I still had nearly an hour before the Big Game Show, so I decided to make a start on Zoe's book. It soon had me rolling about in stitches. It was one of the funniest books I'd ever read. In fact, it was so funny that I forgot the time. When I next looked up, the clock said ten past nine. I'd missed the show!

I found Mum asleep on the sofa. "Why didn't you remind me?" I said. "Now I'll be the only one that didn't watch."

"Tell them you had more important things to do," said Mum. "That would be *really* cool!"

Mum just had no idea at all.

At break the next day, Candy squeaked, "Did you watch, did you watch?"

I screwed up my face. "No!" I moaned. "I couldn't." It had taken me all night to think up an excuse. "You'll never believe it ... we had a power cut!"

"A power cut?" They stared at me like they had never heard of such a thing.

"Weird," said Ivana.

"Tell me about it!" I wailed. "I was, like, freaking out!"

"You don't know what you missed," said Michelle. "You'll never guess who the mystery celeb was!"

I said, "Who, who?"

"It was Andy!"

"*Andeeee!*"

They all giggled and screamed, so I giggled and screamed with them.

"*Andeee*," I moaned. "I missed Andee!"

Andy, the friend of You-Know-Who. But I didn't know who! And I didn't know Andy. I didn't know anything!

I was so angry with myself. And with Zoe. Why did she have to give me that stupid book to read? And then there was Mum? Just sitting there, *sleeping*. I'd told her I wanted to watch the show!

Mum was *so* not cool. Michelle's mum was – I'd seen her. She was, like, totally young, and slim, and always had smart clothes. I think it must be easy to be cool when you have a mum like that. It's not so easy when you have a mum who just falls asleep on the sofa and doesn't care.

"Hey!" Michelle prodded at me. "Are we still on for Saturday?"

I said, "Saturday?" My birthday pizza! I had almost forgotten.

"Are we still on?" said Michelle.

"Yes, of course," I said.

"In that case," said Michelle, "ask your mum if we can go to Mama Angela's. They've got this waiter that looks just like Andy!"

"*Andeee!*"

We screamed again. This time, I screamed louder than anyone.

# Chapter 5
# Big Book of Bloopers

At lunch that day, Zoe came and sat next to me. I felt a bit scared, in case word got back to Michelle. But she and the others were all trying out for parts in the end of term show, so I was on my own. And like I said, you can't *stop* people sitting next to you. It would be rude to just get up and walk away.

"Did you read that book?" said Zoe.

I didn't want to talk about the book. I still felt cross about it.

"Didn't you think it was funny? That bit where her skirt gets caught in the escalator!" Zoe giggled.

I giggled, too. I didn't want to, but I couldn't stop myself. That had been one of the parts which made me roll about and clutch my tummy, I was laughing so much.

I gasped, and mopped at my eyes. "It's when it starts unravelling – "

"And she starts tugging at it – "

"And it all comes to pieces!"

We both howled.

"It's funny when you read about it," I said, "but in real life it would be so embarrassing!"

"Like one time when I went to stay with my cousins," said Zoe, "we went for a walk and I fell into this really yucky pond and had to go home all wet and stinky. I was covered in green gunge!"

"That's not as bad as what happened to me," I said. "I was in the shopping centre with my friend and we went to the loo. When I came out I'd gone and tucked the back of my skirt into my pants so it was all rucked up. I didn't even notice till I saw myself in a shop window!"

"*Oh!*" Zoe clapped her hands to her face. "That must have been *really* embarrassing!"

I said, "Yes, cos there were some boys from my school and they saw me. I don't see how anyone could make *that* funny."

"You could if it was in a book," said Zoe. "You can make anything funny, if it's in a book. Hey!" She prodded me. "You know what? We could write one of our own!"

I stared at her. "Write a book?"

"We could do it together," said Zoe. "It would be fun. We could call it the Big Book of Bloopers!"

I giggled. "What's a blooper?" It sounded rude to me.

"A blooper is something really embarrassing," said Zoe. "We could write about the green gunge, and the pants – "

"And the time I had to give someone this bunch of flowers and I tripped over and squashed them all flat!" I was starting to get into the idea in spite of myself.

"What do you think?" said Zoe. "Shall we do it?"

"Yes," I said, "let's!"

Me and Zoe spent the rest of the lunch hour giggling and making notes. I forgot all about Michelle and the others. I was having too much fun thinking up bloopers! And then the bell rang for afternoon school and I heard myself say, "It's my birthday tomorrow."

I had no idea I was going to say it. The words just came out before I could stop them.

"Many happy returns!" said Zoe. "If you'd told me sooner I'd have sent you a card!"

"That's all right," I said. "I was just wondering ... we're going up the road for a pizza. Would you like to come?"

"Ooh, yes, please," said Zoe. "I'd love to!"

It was only later that I began to get cold feet. What had I done? Michelle had warned me over and over not to let Zoe think she was my friend.

I decided there was only one thing for it. I would have to ring Zoe and say that I was very sorry but I'd messed up. I'd blame it on Mum! I would tell her that Mum had said I could only invite three people and I had invited three already. I didn't want to hurt her, but I really couldn't have her turn up at my birthday meal!

I waited until later in the evening, when Mum was in the bath and couldn't hear me. Then I picked up the phone and rang Zoe's number.

It was Zoe who answered. She said, "Hi, Hannah! Guess what I'm doing? I'm making notes for our blooper book! I've got stacks! I'll bring them with me tomorrow, shall I?"

I said, "Um – yes. Well! The thing is – "

"What time do you want me to get there?" said Zoe. "Mum said she'll bring me. Shall we come to your place or are we going to meet somewhere?"

A blob of sweat splashed off my face and on to the telephone. I opened my mouth to say something, but no sound came out.

"Know what?" said Zoe. "I'm really looking forward to it!"

How could I tell her? I couldn't! I swallowed and said, "Me, too."

I told her that we had booked a table at Mama Angela's for seven o'clock.

"I'll be there!" said Zoe.

I hung up the phone. I felt ashamed of myself. How could I be such a wimp?

Zoe would be there, and so would Michelle. So would Candy and Ivana. All of a sudden I found I was wishing that it could just be me and Zoe. Zoe wasn't cool like Michelle. She wasn't pretty, she wasn't popular. But she was far more fun!

Next evening, Mum and me sat in Mama Angela's and waited for the others to arrive. Mum said I seemed a bit on edge. "You're not worried about anything, are you?"

"I think I might have invited some of the wrong people," I said.

That was when Michelle and the others came through the door. They all hooted and waved as they headed for our table. I could almost *feel* the bottom fall out of my tummy. Mum squeezed my hand.

"We all make mistakes," she whispered.

It was a strange sort of evening. Michelle and the other two did a lot of screaming, and giggling, and flirting with the waiters. Zoe sat and talked to Mum. I did a little bit of screaming and giggling but most of the time I just squirmed and felt uncomfortable. I think I would have felt uncomfortable even if I hadn't asked Zoe to come. I am not, to be honest, a very screamy or giggly sort of person. And I am far too shy to flirt with waiters!

At school the next morning, they all ganged up on me.

"What was all that about?" said Michelle. "What was *she* doing there?"

"The Freak!" said Candy. "Nobody invites the Freak!"

I swallowed. "I do."

"Yeah," said Michelle, "we saw. What I want to know is *why*?"

I took a deep breath. "Because I like her."

I didn't hang around with Michelle and the others any more after that. I started hanging round with Zoe instead. I go round with Zoe all the time, now. We do everything together.

We share secrets, and tell jokes, and giggle quite a lot, as well. Sometimes, we even do a bit of screaming. Not too much; just enough to let the world know that *this is us*. Hannah and Zoe. Real, true friends!

Mum was right: wishes *can* come true.

Our books are tested
for children and young people by
children and young people.

Thanks to everyone who consulted on
a manuscript for their time and effort in
helping us to make our books better
for our readers.